MURDO

Based on *The Railway* ... Awdry

Illustrations by
Robin Davies and Jerry Smith

EGMONT

EGMONT

We bring stories to life

First published in Great Britain in 2006
by Egmont UK Limited
239 Kensington High Street, London W8 6SA
This edition published in 2008
All Rights Reserved

Thomas the Tank Engine & Friends™

CREATED BY BRITT ALLCROFT

HiT entertainment

ISBN 978 1 4052 3490 0

1 3 5 7 9 10 8 6 4 2

Printed in Italy

The Forest Stewardship Council (FSC) is an international, non-governmental organisation dedicated to promoting responsible management of the world's forests. FSC operates a system of forest certification and product labelling that allows consumers to identify wood and wood-based products from well managed forests.

For more information about Egmont's paper buying policy please visit www.egmont.co.uk/ethicalpublishing

For more information about the FSC please visit their website at www.fsc.uk.org

TO THE TRAINS →

This is a story about Murdoch the Tender Engine. When he joined my railway, he thought the other engines talked too much. But he soon realised that they weren't that noisy, after all . . .

Thomas, Harvey and Salty love working at Brendam Docks.

Day and night, day after day, cargo ships arrive at the Docks with goods from all over the world.

This keeps the engines very busy. But sometimes, after working very hard all day, they are so tired that their axles ache.

One day, The Fat Controller decided to bring in a new Tender Engine to help. The new engine was long and he had ten wheels.

"This is Murdoch," said The Fat Controller. "He is going to pull goods on the main line."

"Ahoy, Murdoch!" shouted Salty.

"Welcome, Murdoch!" called Harvey.

"You're the biggest engine I've ever seen!" cried Thomas.

"You're a chatty lot," said Murdoch, quietly.

Murdoch didn't like chatty engines or the noisy Docks. He liked quiet runs through the countryside, with just the noise of his engine and the trucks for company.

Soon, Murdoch was coupled to a long line of heavy trucks. His boiler strained, his wheels started to turn and the mighty engine chuffed away.

But Murdoch didn't puff through the countryside. He puffed through a busy builders' yard, with banging, hammering and drilling all around him!

Murdoch longed for some peace and quiet. But everywhere he went, it was noisy and crowded.

At the end of the day, Murdoch was looking forward to a good night's rest.

But when he got back to the engine sheds, Salty and Harvey were full of questions.

"What's the longest train you've ever pulled?" asked Harvey.

"Have you ever worked in France?" added Salty.

"Please," chuffed Murdoch. "I want some peace and quiet! I don't want to share a shed with chatterboxes."

"No need to be rude!" huffed Harvey.

"We're only being friendly!" steamed Salty.

The next morning, Murdoch collected another long, heavy train.

This time he chuffed into the beautiful countryside. It was splendid. All Murdoch could hear was the gentle rumbling of his wheels and the soothing puffing of his engine.

At last, he had some peace and quiet.

But suddenly, Murdoch's Driver applied the brakes and he screeched to a halt. There were sheep on the track – lots of sheep!

"The sheep escaped from that field," said the Driver.

"Through that broken fence," added the Fireman.

The Driver and the Fireman tried to chase the sheep back into the field.

First this way . . . then that way . . .

They tried everything, but nothing worked. The sheep were bleating louder and louder.

"It's no use," grumbled the Driver.

By now, the Driver and Fireman were very cross and tired.

Then they realised that Murdoch's steam had stopped. "The boiler's got no pressure!" cried the Fireman.

Murdoch's fire had gone out.

"I'll go and phone for help," said the Driver.

The Fat Controller was enjoying his afternoon cup of tea when he got the call.

"Murdoch is in trouble?" he exclaimed. "I'll send help right away."

And The Fat Controller went straight to the engine sheds.

Meanwhile, Murdoch was stuck with all the noisy sheep. He was very unhappy.

The valley wasn't peaceful any more. Murdoch had never heard so much noise.

But at last, the farmer and his dog were beginning to move the sheep away.

"Chatty engines are much better than noisy sheep!" muttered Murdoch.

Just then, Salty and Harvey chuffed into view.

"I'm glad to see you two!" exclaimed Murdoch.

"We'll get you out of here in no time!" cried Salty.

Before long, Harvey and Salty were hooked up to Murdoch. Then, with a heave and a huff, they chuffed out of the valley together.

That night, the engines were back in the sheds.

"Thank you for rescuing me," said Murdoch. "I'm sorry I was cross. I'm pleased to share a shed with you."

"And we're pleased to have you," replied Harvey.

"Aye, we are," added Salty.

Murdoch had found his peace and quiet, at last.

The Thomas Story Library is THE definitive collectio
of stories about Thomas and ALL his friends.

5 more Thomas Story Library titles will be chuffing
into your local bookshop in August 2008!

Jeremy
Hector
BoCo
Billy
Whiff

And there are even more Thomas Story Library books to follow la

So go on, start your Thomas Story Library NOW!

A Fantastic Offer for Thomas the Tank Engine Fans!

In every Thomas Story Library book like this one, you will find a special token. Collect 6 Thomas tokens and we will send you a brilliant Thomas poster, and a double-sided bedroom door hanger! Simply tape a £1 coin in the space above, and fill out the form overleaf.

TO BE COMPLETED BY AN ADULT

To apply for this great offer, ask an adult to complete the coupon below and send it with a pound coin and 6 tokens, to:
THOMAS OFFERS, PO BOX 715, HORSHAM RH12 5WG

☐ Please send a Thomas poster and door hanger. I enclose 6 tokens plus a £1 coin. (Price includes P&P)

Fan's name...

Address...

....Postcode............................

Date of birth..

Name of parent/guardian..

Signature of parent/guardian...